Stampede of the
Giant Reptiles

Dinosaur Cove™

CRETACEOUS

Attack of the
LIZARD KING

Charge of the
THREE-HORNED MONSTER

March of the
ARMOURED BEASTS

Flight of the
WINGED SERPENT

Catching the
SPEEDY THIEF

Stampede of the
GIANT REPTILES

Cretaceous
SURVIVAL GUIDE

JURASSIC

 Rescuing the
PLATED LIZARD

Swimming with the
SEA MONSTER

Tracking the
GIGANTIC BEAST

Escape from the
FIERCE PREDATOR

Finding the
DECEPTIVE DINOSAUR

Assault of the
FRIENDLY FIENDS

Jurassic
SURVIVAL GUIDE

TRIASSIC

 Chasing the
TUNNELLING TRICKSTER

Clash of the
MONSTER CROCS

Rampage of the
HUNGRY GIANTS

Haunting of the
GHOST RUNNERS

Swarm of the
FANGED LIZARDS

Snatched by the
DAWN THIEF

Triassic
SURVIVAL GUIDE

PERMIAN

 Stalking the
FANNED PREDATOR

Shadowing the
WOLF-FACE REPTILES

Saving the
SCALY BEAST

Taming the
BATTLING BRUTES

Snorkelling with the
SAW SHARK

Hunted by the
INSECT ARMY

Permian
SURVIVAL GUIDE

DOUBLE LENGTH ADVENTURES

The
CRETACEOUS CHASE

Lost in the
JURASSIC

Journey to the
ICE AGE

A Cretaceous Adventure

Dinosaur Cove™

Stampede of the
Giant Reptiles

by
REX STONE

illustrated by
MIKE SPOOR

Series created by
Working Partners Ltd

OXFORD
UNIVERSITY PRESS

With special thanks to Jan Burchett and Sara Vogler.
Thank you, also, to Mark Ford of the British and Irish
Meteorite Society for his patient and helpful advice.

For Grandpa Dillon R.S.

These illustrations are for you Christopher.
Enjoy the adventure! M.S.

OXFORD
UNIVERSITY PRESS

Great Clarendon Street, Oxford OX2 6DP
Oxford University Press is a department of the University of Oxford.
It furthers the University's objective of excellence in research, scholarship,
and education by publishing worldwide in

Oxford New York

Auckland Cape Town Dar es Salaam Hong Kong Karachi
Kuala Lumpur Madrid Melbourne Mexico City Nairobi
New Delhi Shanghai Taipei Toronto

With offices in

Argentina Austria Brazil Chile Czech Republic France Greece
Guatemala Hungary Italy Japan Poland Portugal Singapore
South Korea Switzerland Thailand Turkey Ukraine Vietnam

Oxford is a registered trade mark of Oxford University Press
in the UK and in certain other countries

British Library Cataloguing in Publication Data

Data available

ISBN: 978-0-19-279370-6

1 3 5 7 9 10 8 6 4 2

Printed in Italy

Paper used in the production of this book is a natural,
recyclable product made from wood grown in sustainable forests
The manufacturing process conforms to the environmental
regulations of the country of origin

FACT FILE

➡️ JAMIE HAS JUST MOVED FROM THE CITY TO LIVE IN THE LIGHTHOUSE IN DINOSAUR COVE. JAMIE'S DAD IS OPENING A DINOSAUR MUSEUM ON THE BOTTOM FLOOR OF THE LIGHTHOUSE. WHEN JAMIE GOES HUNTING FOR FOSSILS IN THE CRUMBLING CLIFFS ON THE BEACH HE MEETS A LOCAL BOY, TOM, AND THE TWO DISCOVER AN AMAZING SECRET: A WORLD WITH **REAL, LIVE DINOSAURS!** BUT THE BOYS HAVE TO LOOK OUT FOR FALLING ROCKS AND STAMPEDES!

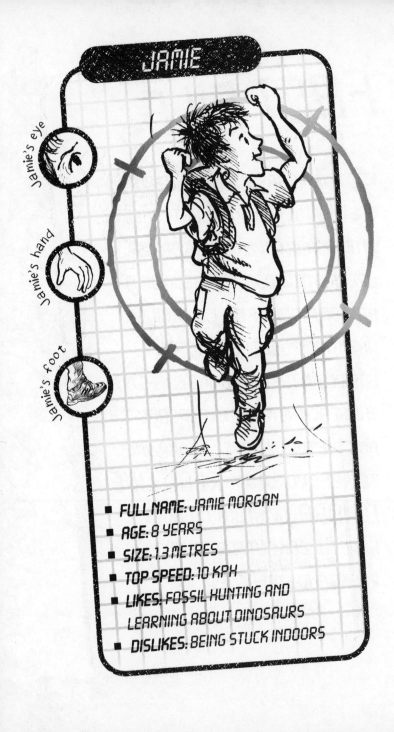

JAMIE

Jamie's eye

Jamie's hand

Jamie's foot

- **FULL NAME:** JAMIE MORGAN
- **AGE:** 8 YEARS
- **SIZE:** 1.3 METRES
- **TOP SPEED:** 10 KPH
- **LIKES:** FOSSIL HUNTING AND LEARNING ABOUT DINOSAURS
- **DISLIKES:** BEING STUCK INDOORS

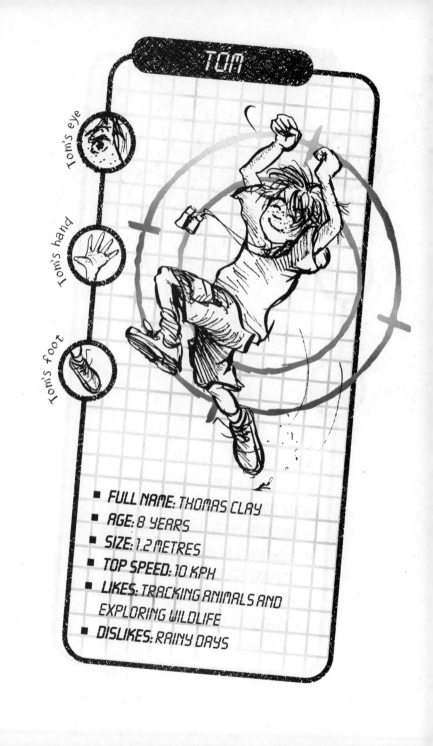

TOM

Tom's eye

Tom's hand

Tom's foot

- **FULL NAME:** THOMAS CLAY
- **AGE:** 8 YEARS
- **SIZE:** 1.2 METRES
- **TOP SPEED:** 10 KPH
- **LIKES:** TRACKING ANIMALS AND EXPLORING WILDLIFE
- **DISLIKES:** RAINY DAYS

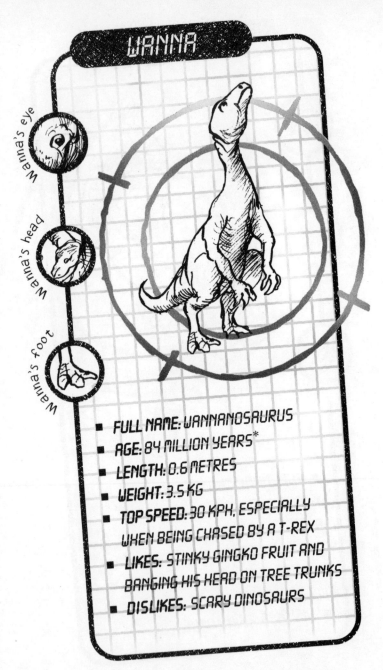

WANNA

Wanna's eye

Wanna's head

Wanna's foot

- FULL NAME: WANNANOSAURUS
- AGE: 84 MILLION YEARS*
- LENGTH: 0.6 METRES
- WEIGHT: 3.5 KG
- TOP SPEED: 30 KPH, ESPECIALLY WHEN BEING CHASED BY A T-REX
- LIKES: STINKY GINGKO FRUIT AND BANGING HIS HEAD ON TREE TRUNKS
- DISLIKES: SCARY DINOSAURS

*NOTE: SCIENTISTS CALL THIS PERIOD THE LATE CRETACEOUS

EDMONTOSAURUS

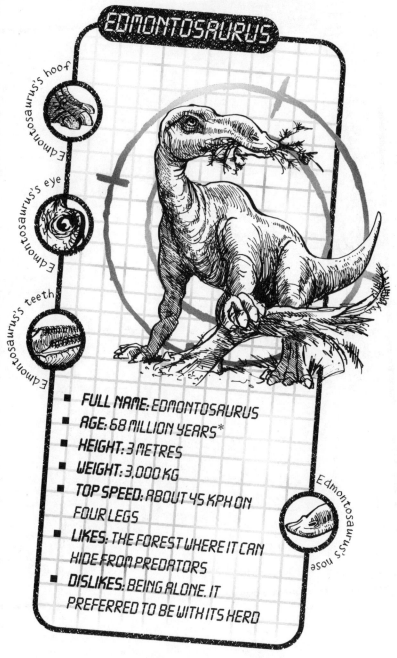

Edmontosaurus's hoof

Edmontosaurus's eye

Edmontosaurus's teeth

Edmontosaurus's nose

- **FULL NAME:** EDMONTOSAURUS
- **AGE:** 68 MILLION YEARS*
- **HEIGHT:** 3 METRES
- **WEIGHT:** 3,000 KG
- **TOP SPEED:** ABOUT 45 KPH ON FOUR LEGS
- **LIKES:** THE FOREST WHERE IT CAN HIDE FROM PREDATORS
- **DISLIKES:** BEING ALONE. IT PREFERRED TO BE WITH ITS HERD

*NOTE: SCIENTISTS CALL THIS PERIOD THE LATE CRETACEOUS

DINOSAUR COVE

Village

Marina

Sealight Head

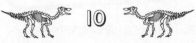

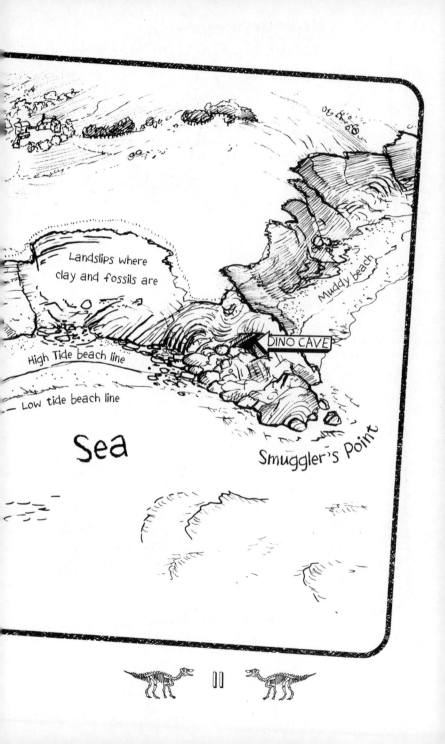

Landslips where
clay and fossils are

Muddy beach

DINO CAVE

High Tide beach line

Low tide beach line

Sea

Smuggler's Point

II

CHAPTER 1

Jamie Morgan stared at the huge
dinosaur towering over him.

'That is awesome!' he exclaimed
to his best friend Tom. 'A life-sized
model of an edmontosaurus skeleton.'

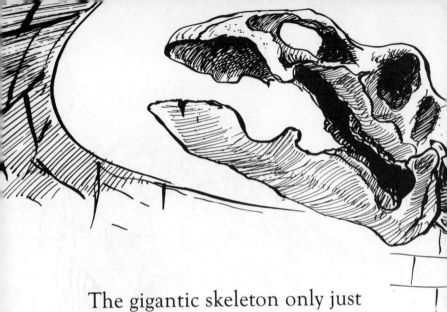

The gigantic skeleton only just
fitted in the museum on the
ground floor of Jamie's lighthouse
home. Its huge tail curled round
the whitewashed walls and it reared
up so that its duck-billed nose was
high over the boys' heads. The
museum was finally ready. A big
banner hung outside the
lighthouse:

**Dinosaur Cove Museum Grand
Opening Today, One O'Clock.**
This was the day everyone had been
waiting for.

FLASH! *FLASH!* *FLASH!*

Jamie and Tom blinked in surprise.
The photographer from the county
paper was aiming her camera at the
edmontosaurus. They jumped aside.

'It's OK, boys,' she called, waving
an arm. 'Let's have you in the shot.
It'll show readers just how big this
beast really was.'

She took picture after picture,
then grabbed Jamie's dad and made

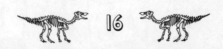

him pose over by the Cretaceous landscape model.

Tom rubbed his eyes. 'I'm seeing stars after all that!'

'But imagine how many photos she'd take if she saw a real live edmontosaurus,' said Jamie.

'We've never seen a real one close up,' said Tom.

'Maybe we will one day,' Jamie whispered.

Jamie and Tom shared an amazing secret. They had discovered Dino World, a land of living dinosaurs, and they visited it whenever they could.

'I wonder why we haven't already seen one,' said Tom.

'This will tell us where to look,' declared Jamie. He turned on his Fossil Finder and typed in: edmontosaurus.

'*HERBIVORE*,' he read from the screen. '*ATE LEAVES AND BRANCHES. SLOW MOVING. WALKED ON ITS BACK LEGS*—just like our model.'

'But where did it live?' asked Tom.

EDMONTOSAURUS

SEARCH: EDMONTOSAURUS

'It says here it kept to the trees to hide from predators. That was its only defence.'

'That explains why we've never seen one,' said Tom, 'if they were always hiding. That should be our next dinosaur mission—hunt the eddie!'

Jamie put the Fossil Finder away in his backpack. He had a gleam in his eye. 'Maybe I could ask if we can have a break?'

Tom grinned. 'Are you thinking what I'm thinking?'

'Time for a trip to Dino World!'

Dad was being photographed next to the triceratops skull so Jamie and Tom

ran up to Grandad. He was frowning at his reflection in a display case.

'Look at me,' he said, before Jamie had a chance to speak. 'Why can't I wear my old jumper and trousers like I do every other day of the year? I feel silly all done up like a dog's dinner.'

'But you look so smart in that suit,

Grandad,' said Jamie. 'No one will look at the exhibits. They'll all be admiring you.'

'Get away!' Grandad laughed

as he straightened his tie. 'They'll just think I'm another fossil. Now what are you two scamps after? Out with it.'

'It's nothing really,' said Jamie casually. 'It's just that, well, the museum's ready now so we were wondering if we could go outside for a while.'

Grandad looked at the ankylosaurus-shaped clock on the wall, showing nine fifteen. 'Don't see why not,' he said. 'As long as you're

21

back sharp at one for the ceremony—clean and tidy.'

'Thanks, Grandad.' Jamie swung his backpack onto his back and hurried out of the lighthouse, Tom right behind him.

They scrambled across the beach and up to the cave entrance high in the cliffs. Making sure no one was in sight, they slipped inside. Jamie dug in his backpack for his torch, but his hand closed around something lumpy and hard.

'Hey, look,' Jamie said, pulling it out along with the torch. 'This is the ammonite I found on my first day in Dinosaur Cove.'

'The first day we discovered Dino World,' Tom remembered.

Jamie tossed the fossil in his backpack and shone the torch on the five fossilized footprints in the stone floor. Every time he saw them he felt the same rush of excitement.

'Let's get back there,' he said. The boys trod in each of the dinosaur prints. One . . . two . . . three . . . four . . . FIVE! The dark cave disappeared and they stepped into the scorching

heat and dazzling light of Dino World.

'It's great to be back!' exclaimed Tom, looking at the huge trees and dense jungle undergrowth around them.

Instead of the usual hum of insects and distant calls of dinosaurs there was an eerie silence.

'Listen!' Jamie said.

Tom listened hard. 'I can't hear a thing.'

'Exactly,' said Jamie. 'Something's not right.'

CHAPTER 2

SEARCH:

ABCDEFGHIJKLMN
OPQRSTUVWXYZ
1234567890

'Wanna!' called Jamie. His voice
sounded strange, echoing through the
silent trees. 'Where are you, Wanna?'

There was no sign of the friendly
little dinosaur who usually came to

greet them. The boys began searching the undergrowth, pushing aside giant tangled creepers.

There was a rustling in a nearby laurel bush. 'What was that?' Jamie stopped. 'Wanna?'

The little wannanosaurus
crept out from between the
leaves, his eyes darting about
nervously. Jamie and Tom rushed
over and hugged him.

'You don't know how
pleased we are to see you,'
said Tom, scratching him
hard on his scaly back.

But Wanna just gave a feeble
grunk.

Tom frowned. 'This isn't like you,
Wanna. What's the matter?'

Jamie reached up into a tree and
picked some orange fruit. 'I know
what you need, boy,' he said. He

tossed one to Wanna and put the others in his backpack.

Wanna looked warily around and then gulped the fruit.

'One thing hasn't changed,' said Jamie. 'Wanna still loves gingkoes.'

'Another thing hasn't changed,' Tom said, holding his nose. 'The gingkoes are still as smelly as ever.'

'But everything else is different.' Jamie frowned. 'Let's find out what's going on.'

With Wanna sticking close to their heels, they made their way through the jungle to a gap in the trees where they could look out over the Great Plains.

The plains lay below them, shimmering in the heat—completely deserted.

'There should be herds of triceratops and hadrosaurs and loads more,' said Tom in disbelief. 'I don't like it.' He pulled out his binoculars and scanned the plains. 'There's nothing moving at all, except the geyser spouts of course. They're still shooting up into the air.'

'What if the dinosaurs are gone?'
whispered Jamie.

Tom looked at him, horrified. 'No,
they must be here somewhere.'

The boys started down the steep
slope of Gingko Hill, but Wanna
hung back, trembling and grunking
anxiously.

'Come on, boy,' called Jamie,
holding out a gingko from his bag.

The little dinosaur crept forward
and ate the fruit. He didn't leave
their side as they trampled through
the hot, damp undergrowth, and
jumped the stepping stones over
the river.

'This silence is really strange,' said Jamie in a low voice.

'And I've never seen Wanna like this before,' said Tom. 'Not even when we met the t-rex!'

Suddenly, there was a deafening crash overhead.

BANG!

The boys ducked instinctively.

BANG!

Another one. The boys dived to the ground, covering their heads with their hands. Wanna disappeared under a cluster of spiky flowers.

Jamie raised his head. 'There's no way that was a dinosaur!' he whispered. 'Not even a t-rex could make that much noise.'

'So what could it be?' Tom asked.

CHAPTER 3

Jamie and Tom scrambled to their feet.
'We've got to find out what that was,'
muttered Jamie. 'Here, Wanna!'

A terrified Wanna crept out from
the leaves of his hiding place. The

three friends walked through the last
few trees and out onto the plains.

'Look at that!' gasped Tom.

Two blinding lights, as bright as
the sun, were scorching through the
sky over the Far Away Mountains.

'Meteors!' gasped Jamie, screening
his eyes from the glare.

The boys watched as
the glowing objects
shot towards the
middle of

the plains like
supersonic jets.
They left long dazzling
trails behind them.

'They're falling to earth!'
yelled Jamie. 'And fast.'

'They're going to hit the
plains,' shouted Tom.

BOOM!
BOOM!

There was a dreadful
noise like cannon

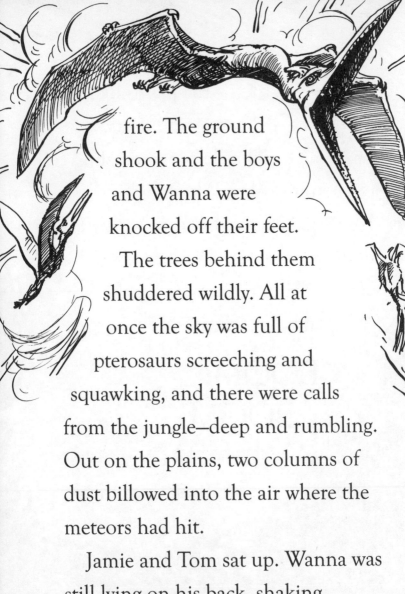

fire. The ground
shook and the boys
and Wanna were
knocked off their feet.
The trees behind them
shuddered wildly. All at
once the sky was full of
pterosaurs screeching and
squawking, and there were calls
from the jungle—deep and rumbling.
Out on the plains, two columns of
dust billowed into the air where the
meteors had hit.

Jamie and Tom sat up. Wanna was
still lying on his back, shaking.

'Cool!' said Jamie. 'We've just seen a meteor strike!'

'And felt it!' said Tom, getting up and gently pulling Wanna to his feet. 'No wonder he was so nervous and all the dinosaurs are hiding. They must have sensed the danger.'

The boys scanned the plains from Fang Rock right round to the cliffs of the White Ocean. There were still no creatures to be seen. Even the pterosaurs had disappeared again.

A look of horror came over Tom's face. 'Don't some people say that it was a meteor that killed the dinosaurs millions of years ago?

 41

Do you think that's going to happen here?'

'No,' said Jamie firmly. 'That one was so huge that it created a massive dust cloud and blocked out the sun. These haven't. But we can find out more about them.' He pulled out his Fossil Finder and tapped in: *METEOR*. Then he read, *'A LUMP OF ROCK FROM SPACE THAT HITS THE EARTH'S ATMOSPHERE WITH A SONIC BOOM...'*

'That must have been the bangs we heard when we were in the jungle,' nodded Tom.

'AND STREAKS ACROSS THE SKY WITH A BRIGHT GLOW,' Jamie continued.

'*THE ONES THAT HIT THE EARTH ARE CALLED METEORITES*. Look: here are some awesome pictures.'

He showed Tom.

'Wow!' Tom said. 'We could actually see real meteorites—just after they've landed!'

'I've always wanted to see a space rock,' said Jamie. 'Let's head for those dust clouds.'

The boys left the jungle behind them and set off across the vast, grassy plains. Wanna scampered along, looking happier now.

'They've landed a lot further away than I thought,' said Tom. 'One of

43

the dust clouds is right at the foot of the Far Away Mountains—near that pine forest.'

'Then we'll head for the closer one,' said Jamie, 'near where the geysers are.' He pulled out the map they'd made of Dino World. 'That's where we chased the velociraptor.'

'Well, I hope he's not still lurking around!' Tom checked his compass. 'We should head north-west,' he said.

'Shouldn't we be seeing the waterspouts gushing up then?' Jamie shielded his eyes as he peered forward. 'All I can see is steam.'

'The dust must be hiding them,'

said Tom. He held an imaginary microphone. 'And here's Tom Clay taking you on a quest to find the supersonic space rocks that have spooked all the creatures of Dino World.'

'I wonder what Tom Clay has to say about the ground ahead.' Jamie said, pointing.

'It's black!' Tom gasped. 'I mean . . . Now we

can clearly see the effects of this
meteor strike. We are entering
the blast area now. All around
the vegetation is singed and . . .
Wow! I can feel the heat through
my trainers.'

The boys walked gingerly across
the blackened earth.

'You're right,' said Jamie.
'It is hot! Look at poor Wanna.
He could do with some shoes.'

Their little dino friend was hopping from side to side trying not to get his feet burnt.

'Look!' Tom said, as they came nearer the site of the strike. 'There are little fires all around us.'

Small plants were crackling, sending sparks into the air. A spark landed on a dry bush nearby and it

burst into flames. Wanna
skittered off in alarm.

'It's OK, Wanna,' said Tom.
'Stick with us and you'll be fine.'

'The fires will probably
have scared off the raptor,' Jamie
guessed.

'Good thing for us, because we
don't have any bacon to distract
it,' Tom said.

The air was becoming very steamy.
'We should have reached the
geysers by now,' said Jamie. 'But why
can't we hear the water spouting?'

Cautiously the boys stepped
forward through the steam and saw a
huge, gaping hole.

'This is where the geysers should be,' Tom said.

They peered over the rim of the pit and Jamie's feet dislodged stones which tumbled into the bottomless dark. They could hear hissing and rumbling deep underground.

'It's like being on the edge of a cliff,' breathed Tom. 'The ground's just . . . vanished!'

'The meteorite has destroyed the geysers,' said Jamie in amazement.

'That's some power,' said Tom. 'It must have smashed through the underground caverns where the water

heats up. Now the geysers can't spout up any more.'

'The hole looks as wide as a football pitch,' said Jamie. 'And who knows how deep.'

Grunk-shoo!

Wanna was sniffing at the edge, sneezing as the steam went up his nose. There was a sound of shifting stones and the ground beneath his feet began to crumble. Earth spilled down into the darkness.

'Get back, Wanna!' cried Tom in alarm. 'It's not safe.'

But it was too late. With a horrible crack, the edge gave way. Wanna

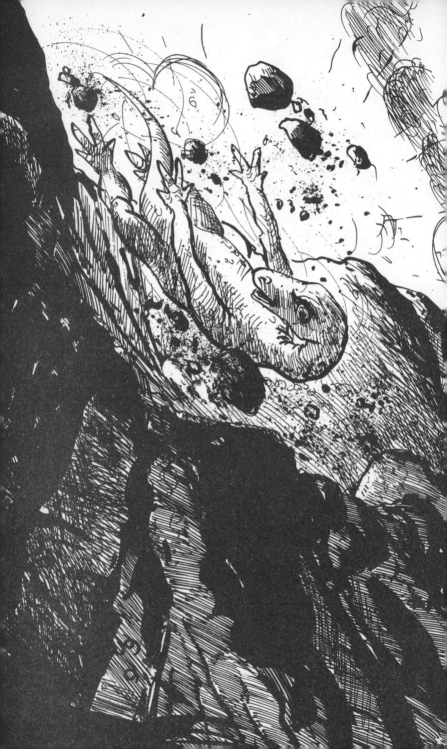

didn't even have time to grunk
before he disappeared into the
deep, cavernous hole.

'Wanna!' yelled Tom.

CHAPTER 4

Jamie dropped to his hands and
knees and edged towards the place
where Wanna had disappeared.
He felt the hot steam on his face as
he peered into the blackness. Had
they lost their faithful friend?

'Wanna?' Jamie called out tentatively into the dark chasm.

Grunk. The response was soft and frightened, but relief flooded through Jamie. Wanna was still alive!

'I can see him!' Jamie yelled. 'He's stuck on a sort of rock shelf.'

'We've got to rescue him!' Tom exclaimed.

Jamie took off his backpack and lay down on his stomach. 'I'll try to reach him.'

Tom held his friend's ankles as Jamie leaned carefully over the hole. Through the steam Jamie could just see Wanna, cowering on the ledge,

his eyes wide and terrified. Beyond
him was nothing but the dark of
the deep, steaming pit.

Quick as lightning,
Jamie made a grab for
him. His fingers closed
around one front leg.
'Got him!'

He felt Tom pulling
hard on his ankles and
Jamie clung to Wanna

with all his strength. Wanna
scrabbled on the side of the rock
wall, trying to help. Slowly and surely
Jamie and Tom hauled Wanna up
out of the pit. At last, the three of
them lay sprawled on the ground.

'That was close,' Tom said.

The little dinosaur darted between
his rescuers, licking their faces.

'I think he's saying thank you.'
Jamie grinned.

Grunk, grunk!

Wanna seemed to agree.

'We're not going to find any
meteorites in that steam hole,' said
Tom. 'Let's check out the other

landing site.' He pointed to the dust cloud which was still hovering over the trees at the foot of the Far Away Mountains.

'We haven't been that way before,' said Jamie. 'We'll be able to add what we find to the map.'

'Good idea,' said Tom, checking his compass. 'We're heading north of the geysers, or what's left of them.'

Skirting carefully round the huge pit, the boys set off with Wanna, heading straight towards the Far Away Mountains. As they got closer, the ground around became rougher. They had to step over mossy rocks

 59

to reach the blackened earth of
the second strike. More plants were
crackling around them and they
could see that the trees nestling at
the foot of the mountains had been
scorched by the blast. There were
small fires burning amongst the
broken branches.

'On with our mission,' said Jamie.
'Meteorite, here we come.'

'There's the crater,' said Tom. He
pointed to a dip in the ground
about twenty metres ahead.

'Yay!' Jamie hurried
towards it. It was a

perfect saucer shape. In the centre
lay a jagged black rock, glinting
in the sun.

Jamie punched the air. 'It's the
meteorite!'

They slid down the gentle slope to the gleaming space rock.

'Awesome!' Tom cheered.

Jamie gingerly reached out a finger to touch the surface. 'It's cold!' he said in surprise. He flicked open the Fossil Finder. *'METEORITES,'* he read. *'FRAGMENTS OF ROCK THAT FALL TO EARTH FROM SPACE. THEY CAN MEASURE FROM A GRAIN OF SAND UP TO A FOOTBALL FIELD.'*

'Wow!' gasped Tom. 'I'm glad this one's not as big as that!' He tried to lift it but it didn't budge. 'It's amazing that it's cold when everything else around here is scorched.'

Jamie scanned his Fossil Finder. 'It says the meteor is only hot when it enters the atmosphere and will have cooled down by the time it reaches the ground. The fires around are caused by the impact when it hits.'

They examined the rock closely. 'It's got shiny pieces of metal in it,' said Tom, running his hand over it. 'And holes like space worms have burrowed through it.'

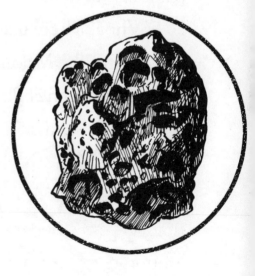

'Just think,' said Jamie, jumping on top of the rock. 'Less than an hour ago this was hurtling through the galaxy!'

Tom joined him. 'Here's Tom Clay and Jamie Morgan, famous explorers, whizzing past the stars on their own personal meteor.'

'Whoa! There goes Mars!'

'Mind the Moon!'

'Here comes Planet Earth. Crash!'

Jamie jumped off the meteorite and threw himself onto the dusty floor of the crater. Wanna grunked round him, enjoying the fun.

'I'm off to Saturn!' Tom announced from the meteorite. 'Hang on, what's that?' he said seriously, balancing on tiptoe.

'I can see a dinosaur!' He asked Jamie to pass up the binoculars and then peered towards the distant trees which were still smouldering from the meteor strike.

Jamie climbed up beside him. 'What is it?'

Tom handed him the binoculars. 'Take a look.'

Jamie aimed them at the trees. 'Wow!' He focused on a flat, wide dinosaur head with a beak-shaped snout and let out a low whistle. 'It's an edmontosaurus—a real live one!'

CHAPTER 5

Jamie scrambled out of the crater and swept the binoculars along the line of pine trees. 'There's a whole herd of edmontosaurs!' he exclaimed. 'They're massive!'

'Cool,' Tom said, hurrying to join him.

The great lumbering dinosaurs were huddled together at the edge of the forest. They took nervous steps on their hind legs towards the smouldering trees and then skittered back in alarm.

'But they don't belong in the open.' Tom looked worried. 'That forest must be their home.'

'Looks like they're too scared to go

back in,' said Jamie, returning
the binoculars to Tom. 'Some of
those branches are still on fire.'

Tom trained the binoculars on an

edmontosaurus at the edge of the group and chuckled. 'I think that one's posing for us!'

The eddie lifted its head up and sniffed the air. It opened its mouth, showing rows and rows of flat teeth.

'Those gnashers would make short work of a tree branch,' Jamie murmured. 'Dad told me they could have up to a thousand teeth!'

'I wouldn't like to be a dino dentist.' Tom laughed. 'You'd need a drill the size of a cricket bat.'

'And buckets of mouthwash.'

'And half your patients would want to eat you!'

'I wish we could get a bit closer,' said Jamie. 'Have we got time?'

Tom looked at his watch. 'Not really. We'd better go. We'll be in big trouble if we're late back for the Grand Opening. Come on, Wanna.'

They began the long walk back towards the geyser crater and the jungle beyond.

'I wish we could tell Dad that we've seen some real edmontosaurs,' sighed Jamie. He turned to get one last look at the eddies and stopped dead.

'Oh no!' he said. 'Look at the flames! The whole forest is alight now!'

Fierce flickers of fire were shooting
up into the sky from the treetops.

'The eddies don't like it,' said
Tom, 'and I don't blame them. Their
home's burning.'

The dinosaurs were backing off
from the trees, buffeting each other
in their fear. The boys could hear
their deep anxious calls.

Suddenly a flaming tree trunk crashed down, hitting the ground in a shower of sparks.

With a terrified bellow, the herd reared away and began to run from the burning trees. Soon the run became a charge. The ground churned under their pounding feet and dust flew up round them.

'They're stampeding,' yelled Tom. 'And they're heading right for us.'

'We better get out of the way, and fast,' Jamie said. 'Come on, Wanna!'

The boys and their dinosaur friend sprinted at full speed back the way they had come, trying to put some distance between them and the frightened dinosaurs. Soon they had to dodge the small fires that still burned here and there in the blast area from the first meteorite.

Jamie turned to see that the
eddies were still stampeding towards
them. 'Wait a minute!' he shouted.
'If the eddies keep running this way,
they'll fall into the geyser pit.'

Tom slowed down, panting. 'We
can't let that happen!'

'We've got to stop them or turn
them away somehow,' said Jamie.

'We could wave our T-shirts at
them,' Tom suggested.

'Too small,' answered Jamie.

'But we haven't got anything else,' Tom said, worried.

'Yes, we have,' said Jamie, running over to a burning bush. 'We'll use fire. That's what

scared them into stampeding in
the first place. We'll stand in
front of the pit and wave
burning branches.'

'Brilliant!' said
Tom. 'Let's do it.'

Wanna butted their legs as if to keep them away from the danger.

'No, Wanna,' said Jamie. 'We've got to do this.' He broke off two crackling branches and held them high. Wanna backed away, grunking in alarm. 'Sorry, little friend,' he said soothingly, 'but it's up to us to save the eddies.'

The boys rushed over to the pit, then turned and faced the oncoming charge.

Jamie could feel sparks from the burning branches stinging his arms but he wasn't going to give up. The terrified edmontosaurs were

thundering towards them, churning up the dust.

The drumming of giant hooves was making the ground shudder. Jamie looked over his shoulder to see a large crack appear near his feet.

CRASH!

A great chunk of earth disappeared into the darkness. Now the edge of the pit was right behind them. If the crack got any wider, the boys would fall into the pit themselves.

'The eddies have to stop!' shouted Jamie desperately. 'It's their only chance—and ours!'

Jamie and Tom waved the burning branches as hard as they could.

But the edmontosaurs were surging on, pounding away on all fours. They were so close the boys

could see their eyes, wide with fear, and their nostrils flaring in panic.

'It's not working,' cried Tom.

'We can't give up!' Jamie shouted.

The stampeding herd was only metres away now. Was it too late? Were they all going to plunge into the crater?

'STOP!' Jamie and Tom bellowed desperately.

At the last minute, the eddies seemed to notice the fire. The leading dinosaurs reared up in terror and swerved away from the geyser pit. The rest of the herd followed, thundering past, throwing dust into the boys' faces.

'We saved them!' yelled Tom.

Grunk, grunk! Wanna appeared and scampered over.

'I agree, Wanna,' Jamie said. 'That was a close shave.'

'Those eddies used all four legs to gallop,' said Tom. 'No wonder they got up such a speed.'

'That's what we'd better do,' said Jamie, looking at his watch, 'if we're going to be in time for the Grand Opening.'

They hurried back towards the jungle. Wanna was his old self, scurrying between them, running ahead and grunking happily all the time.

'At least we got to see a real meteorite,' said Jamie. 'And you got your wish, Tom.'

'What was that?' Tom was puzzled.

'You wanted to see an edmontosaurus close up, remember?'

'I didn't mean that close!' Tom grinned.

They climbed back up Gingko Hill. Wanna waggled his tail in delight as they went.

'He knows there'll be a nice treat waiting for him,' Tom added.

When they reached the cave, they took one more look out over Dino World. A herd of triceratops was

87

grazing by the lagoon and hadrosaurs were plodding down to the river by Fang Rock. Pterosaurs lazily circled in the air. They all seemed to know that the danger was over.

'We mustn't forget to change our map when we get back,' said Tom. 'The geysers have gone and there's that new crater. And the eddies' trees, of course.'

Jamie took the binoculars and
focused on the eddies' trees which
were still burning. 'I hope the fire
doesn't spread or we'll be making
even more changes.'

'I don't think it will,' said Tom.
'Look.' Away in the distance storm

clouds were gathering over the
mountains. 'The rain will soon put
the fire out.'

The boys hurried into the cave and
Wanna followed.

Grunk, grunk! Wanna stared at
them sadly for a moment as if he
didn't want them to go.

'Don't worry, Wanna,' Tom said,
patting him on his hard head. 'We'll
be back soon.'

Jamie gave him the last of the
gingkoes and Wanna cheered up,
gobbling up the treats. Jamie and
Tom waved goodbye and stepped
backwards into the dinosaur

footprints and found themselves back in Dinosaur Cove. They scrambled down to the beach.

Then Tom stopped. 'We can't go to the Grand Opening like this. We're filthy.'

'You're right. Grandad will have a fit,' said Jamie, 'and I don't know what Dad will do—explode probably.'

'Quick,' said Tom. 'We'll have a wash in the sea.'

They hurriedly scrubbed the grime off their arms, legs, and faces and made a dash for the lighthouse. The distant church clock was striking one.

It looked as if the whole village
had come to the Grand Opening,
and crowds of tourists too. A queue
stretched away down the path.

 92

'Our clothes will have to do,'
muttered Jamie as they made their
way past the line of people. 'We've
got no more time. Hopefully
everyone will be too busy looking at
the museum to notice.'

Then they heard a loud voice.
'That edmontosaurus would be an
easy target!' A boy of about fifteen
was looking at a poster for the
museum, showing the eddie model.
He seemed to be telling his friend
all about dinosaurs. 'They were
slow plodders, believe me. Anything
could eat them if they wanted. Bet
they couldn't run.'

'Are you sure?' his friend asked.

'Of course I'm sure,' said the boy.
'I know everything there is to know
about dinosaurs.'

Tom looked at Jamie. 'You tell
him,' he whispered.

'Excuse me,' said Jamie politely.

94

'But the edmontosaurus could get up quite a speed by running on all four legs. It wasn't always an easy target.'

'How do you know?' demanded the boy.

'I've seen—' Jamie stopped himself and quickly recovered. 'I've seen the edmontosaurus skeleton inside. Have a look when you go in. Its front limbs were definitely long enough to run on.'

The boy stared at him open-mouthed.

Tom and Jamie saw Grandad waving them over. They marched up to the front of the queue and up

onto the little stage to stand with
Jamie's dad.

'Welcome to the Dinosaur Cove
Museum,' Mr Morgan began. 'The
most magical dinosaur place in the
whole world . . . '

Jamie smiled a huge smile. He was
proud of his dad's new museum but
nothing compared to Dino World.

'The second most magical place,'
Jamie whispered to Tom.

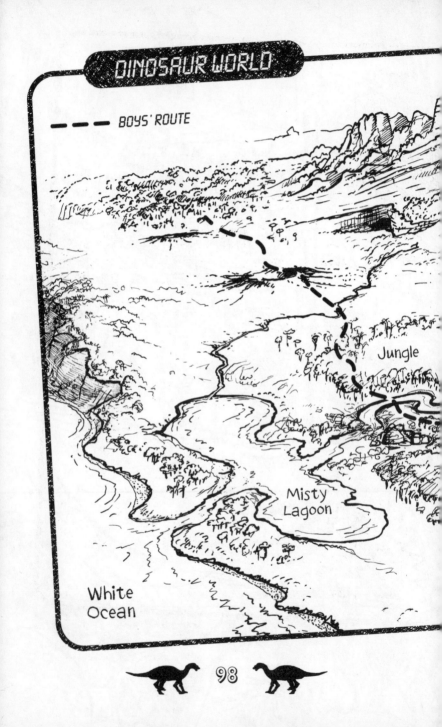

DINOSAUR WORLD

––– BOYS' ROUTE

Jungle

Misty
Lagoon

White
Ocean

98

Far Away Mountains

Great
Plains

Fang
Rock

Crashing
Rock
Falls

Gingko
Hill

GLOSSARY

Ammonite (am-on-ite) – an extinct animal with octopus-like legs and often a spiral-shaped shell that lived in the ocean.

Edmontosaurus (ed-mon-tow-sor-us) – a plant-eating, usually slow-moving dinosaur that walked on its back two legs. Named after the place it was discovered in southern Alberta, Canada.

Geyser (gee-ser) – a hot spring, heated by volcanic activity below the earth's surface, that erupts in a tall stream of hot water and steam, sometimes on a regular schedule.

Gingko (gink-oh) – a tree native to China called a 'living fossil' because fossils of it have been found dating back millions of years, yet they are still around today. Also known as the stink bomb tree because of its smelly apricot-like fruit.

Hadrosaur (had-ro-sor) – a duck-billed dinosaur. This plant eater had a toothless beak but hundreds of teeth in their cheeks.

Meteor (meet-e-or) – matter from outer space that glows when falling through the earth's atmosphere.

Meteorite (meet-e-or-ite) – a meteor that lands on the earth's surface.

Pterosaur (ter-oh-sor) – a prehistoric flying reptile. Its wings were leathery and light and some of these 'winged lizards' had fur on their bodies and bony crests on their heads.

Triceratops (t-tops) (try-serra-tops) – a three-horned, plant-eating dinosaur which looks like a rhinoceros.

Wannanosaurus (wah-nan-oh-sor-us) – a dinosaur that only ate plants and used its hard, flat skull to defend itself. Named after the place it was discovered: Wannano in China.

Come and meet me . . .
in a Jurassic adventure

Turn the page
to read the
first chapter of the
next adventure in the

Dinosaur Cove™

series:

Resucing the
Plated Lizard

'Dino World here we come!'

Jamie Morgan and his best friend, Tom Clay, clattered down the stairs of the old lighthouse ready for a new adventure. They burst into the museum on the ground floor and skidded to a halt in front of Jamie's dad.

'It's good to hear you being so enthusiastic about the museum,' Jamie's dad said. He was kneeling on the floor beside a sandpit, arranging plastic trowels around the edge.

Jamie spluttered. 'Er um . . . it's awesome!' He hadn't been talking about his dad's fantastic dinosaur museum. He'd meant the secret world of real dinosaurs that he and Tom had discovered in a hidden cave.

'Visitors will love your new exhibit,' Tom said to change the subject. He took a trowel and poked at a cookie-sized fossil half-buried in the sand. 'That's an ammonite.'

'If you dig it out and match it with the ammonites on display you can find out what time period it comes from,' Mr Morgan told him.

Permian

Triassic

Jurassic

Cretaceous

Jamie looked into the glass display case against the wall. Each ammonite fossil was carefully labelled with time periods, including Permian, Triassic, Jurassic, and Cretaceous.

Jamie started rummaging in his backpack. 'Can you tell when my ammonite is from?' he asked, pulling out the one he'd found on his first day on the beach in Dinosaur Cove.

Jamie's dad studied the fossil closely and checked it against the ones in the display case. 'It has deep ridges and the ribs are complete circles around the outer edge. That means it's definitely Late Cretaceous.'

Jamie smiled at Tom. Their secret cave led to a world with real, live Late Cretaceous dinosaurs like triceratops and velociraptors.

'Ammonites are like keys to the past,' Jamie's dad went on. 'Scientists use them to help date the rock layers where they're found.'

'Cool,' Tom said.

'We're going exploring,' Jamie said. 'You can keep my ammonite for the exhibit.'

'Thanks, son.' Jamie's dad buried it under the sand with the other ammonites. 'Have fun!'

'We will.'

Jamie and Tom dashed out of the lighthouse and ran as fast as they could along the beach and up the cliff to the old smugglers' cave.

'I can't wait to see Wanna again,' Tom said as they wriggled through the gap at the back of the cave into the secret chamber. They'd met the wannanosaurus on their first trip to

Dino World
and the little
dinosaur had
been their friend
ever since. It was
actually their dinosaur friend's
fossilized footprints that had
transported them into Dino World.

'Any second now . . .' Jamie could
feel the excitement bubbling up
inside him as he put his feet into
Wanna's fossilized footprints. What
dinosaurs would they meet today?

'One, two, three . . .' Jamie headed towards the rock face. 'Four, five—OUCH!' Instead of emerging into Dino World, Jamie smacked into the solid rock.

Tom bumped into the back of him. 'What happened?'

Jamie rubbed his scraped knee. 'I don't know.' He shone his torch on the fossil footprints.

'You must be doing it wrong,' Tom said. 'Let me go first.' He took five confident steps and then his head whacked against the cave wall. 'OW!' he yelled, rubbing his forehead. 'It's not working!'

Jamie fought
down a wave of panic.
'We must be doing something
different.'

'We're walking like we always
do and wearing what we always
wear,' Tom said. 'What's in your
backpack?'

Jamie tipped out the contents
and shone his torch on them. 'Fossil
Finder, compass, map, binoculars,

sandwiches.' He stuffed everything back in.

'Even the sandwiches are the same—cheese and your grandad's pickle.' Tom sighed.

'But something must have changed,' Jamie insisted.

'Maybe something's missing,' Tom said.

'My ammonite!' Jamie jumped to his feet. 'It's been with us every time we've been to Dino World. We've got to get it back!'

They raced to the old lighthouse and the main door was still shut. The museum hadn't yet opened for the day.

'We're in luck,' Tom said as Jamie pulled open the heavy door. They tiptoed into the museum and peered cautiously around.

'There's no sign of Dad. Quick!' Jamie and Tom each grabbed a trowel and dug in the sand. Soon, they each had a big pile of ammonites to look through.

'That's the lot.' Jamie put down his trowel and started looking through

the fossils. 'My ammonite is black
with shiny gold ridges, and it's about
as big as a yo-yo.'

'We should put the wrong ones
back,' Tom suggested.

'Good idea,' Jamie agreed. They
reburied the fossils that were too big
or too small or made of the wrong
type of stone until only two
were left.

'Which one is it?'
Tom asked, looking at
the two similar fossils.

'It's hard to tell,'
Jamie said, 'but I think
it's this one.'

Tom agreed and Jamie stuffed the ammonite he was holding into his pocket whilst Tom pushed the other one back into the sandpit. They slipped out of the door and ran back to the cave as fast as they could.

'Fingers crossed.' Jamie fitted his feet into Wanna's fossilized footprints. 'One, two, three . . .' He walked slowly towards the wall, bracing himself for impact with the solid rock. 'Four . . .' Jamie held his hands out in front of him as he stepped forward. 'Five!'

He felt a sudden rush of hot, humid air and his ears rang with the calls of strange jungle creatures. He took a deep breath and his nostrils filled with the peaty smell of warm leaf-mould. Jamie opened his eyes. Tom was standing next to him. They were back in Dino World.

'Hurrah!' Tom shouted.

Jamie looked behind him to check that their usual way home

was there and was relieved to see
the muddy version of the fossilized
footprints leading away from the back
of the cave.

'Everything is back to normal,'
Jamie declared. 'Let's go!' Jamie and
Tom dashed out of the cave and set
off through the gingko trees.

Jamie parted the creepers and
stopped dead. 'What happened to
the view?'

Tom's mouth dropped open. 'I have
no idea.'

The hillside view over the grassy
plains, the winding river, Fang
Rock, and Far Away Mountains had

disappeared. Instead, all they could see was the trunks of more jungle trees. Dino World had changed!

Join Jamie and Tom in **Dino World** with the

Dinosaur Cove™

CRETACEOUS SURVIVAL GUIDE

Turn the page for a taster of all the **awesome** things to do . . .

Create!

MAKE YOUR OWN EDIBLE DINO POO!

YOU WILL NEED:

- 100g plain chocolate
- 50g margarine
- 2 tablespoons golden syrup
- 150g plain digestive biscuits

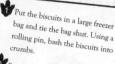

1 Put the biscuits in a large freezer bag and tie the bag shut. Using a rolling pin, bash the biscuits into crumbs.

2 Break up the chocolate into pieces and put them in a saucepan. Heat the pan on a low temperature until the chocolate has melted.

Don't forget to ask a grown-up to help melt the chocolate!

3 Stir the margarine and syrup into the melted chocolate.

4 Take the saucepan off the heat. Pour the biscuit crumbs into the chocolate mixture and stir together.

Play!

WHICH CRETACEOUS DINO ARE YOU?

START
Do you walk on two legs or four legs?

Two legs — Super speedy or supremely strong?

Strong — Hunt on land or in the air?
- Land → T-Rex
- Air → Quetzalcoatlus

Speedy — Carnivore or herbivore?
- Carnivore → Velociraptor
- Herbivore → Wannanosaurus

Four legs — Super speedy or supremely strong?

Speedy — Up high or down low?
- Down low → Bagaceratops
- Up high → Edmontosaurus

Strong — Protected by horns or bony armour?
- Horns → Triceratops
- Bony armour → Ankylosaurus

Discover!

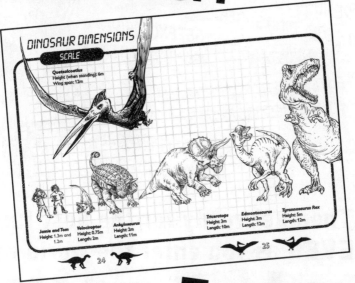

DINOSAUR DIMENSIONS

SCALE

Quetzalcoatlus
Height (when standing): 6m
Wing span: 12m

Jamie and Tom
Height: 1.3m and 1.2m

Velociraptor
Height: 0.75m
Length: 2m

Ankylosaurus
Height: 2m
Length: 11m

Triceratops
Height: 3m
Length: 10m

Edmontosaurus
Height: 3m
Length: 12m

Tyrannosaurus Rex
Height: 5m
Length: 12m

Explore!

T-REX: THE LIZARD KING

Tyrannosaurus Rex was a carnivore that ate all sorts of other creatures, from small dinosaurs like velociraptors to large ones like edmontosaurs. Palaeontologists think the t-rex was probably a scavenger as well as a hunter, eating up the remains of creatures that had already died. With chisel-shaped teeth at the front and huge teeth with knife-like serrated edges filling the rest of its mouth, the t-rex was a fearsome predator. The biggest t-rex skull ever found is 150cm long and was discovered in the 1960s. The biggest and best preserved whole t-rex skeleton is in the Field Museum of Natural History in Chicago. Its name is FMNH PR 2081, but its nickname is Sue.

We found out that competition for food was fierce in the Cretaceous period when we ran into not one but **two** t-rexes! We'd only just managed to escape one dino's snapping jaws when we stumbled into a battle between two of the massive lizard kings.